BRIAN SIBLEY BRINGS ALIVE

The Magical World of
NARNIA

For
ANDREW, STEPHEN, PAUL and ANNA
and their father
GEOFFREY MARSHALL TAYLOR
who has brought the
World of Narnia
alive on radio

First published in Lions 1990
Lions is an imprint of the Children's Division,
part of the Harper Collins Publishing Group,
8 Grafton Street, London W1X 3LA

Copyright text © C. S. Lewis Pte Ltd and Brian Sibley 1990
Copyright illustrations © Pauline Baynes and Pauline King 1990

Printed in Great Britain by BPCC Paulton Books Limited

Conditions of Sale
This book is sold subject to the condition that it shall not, by way
of trade or otherwise, be lent, re-sold, hired out or otherwise
circulated without the publisher's prior consent in any form of
binding or cover other than that in which it is published and
without a similar condition including this condition being
imposed on the subsequent purchaser.

BRIAN SIBLEY BRINGS ALIVE

The Magical World of NARNIA

LIONS

Acknowledgements

A lot of people have helped the author in creating *The Magical World Of Narnia* and without their imaginative contributions this book could never have been put together. Rosemary Sandberg gave continuous enthusiastic encouragement and Pauline Baynes graciously allowed the use of her wonderful illustrations from the Chronicles of Narnia. The additional drawings are by Pauline King; Ruth Thomson contributed the masks, diagrams and some of the games and puzzles; the music is by John Miles and the delicious recipes are by Lucinda de la Rue; the book's design is the work of Ian Butterworth and Heather Garioch. Lastly (and from the very beginning) there was Rosemary Stones, who brought all these people together and then skilfully edited their ideas into a book.

You may perform the plays in this book and any plays you make up yourselves from the Narnia stories for your friends and families but you may not put on any kind of public performance at which you charge for admission.

Brian Sibley

Contents

About This Book

It took a remarkable imagination to create the magical world of Narnia, but C. S. Lewis had always been good at imagining strange and wonderful things. Even when he was still quite a young boy, he wrote stories and poems, made up plays and drew pictures of curious creatures and maps of imaginary lands.

When he grew up, he continued using his vivid imagination to tell unforgettable stories. Some of these were about spaceships travelling to Mars and Venus, others were about the enchanted land of Narnia behind the wardrobe door.

C. S. Lewis's stories began with pictures. One idea came from a picture he saw in his mind "of a faun carrying an umbrella and parcels in a snowy wood". He explained: "This picture had been in my mind since I was about sixteen. Then one day, when I was forty, I said to myself, 'Let's try and make a story about it'." That story, of course, was *The Lion, the Witch and the Wardrobe* and it was the first of the seven Chronicles of Narnia to be written. The other books in the series are *The Magician's Nephew, The Horse and His*

Boy, Prince Caspian, *The Voyage of the* Dawn Treader, *The Silver Chair* and *The Last Battle.*

Many years later, whenever C. S. Lewis's young readers used to ask if he was going to write any more stories, he used to reply: "I'm afraid I've said all I have to say about Narnia, but why don't you try to write one yourself?"

Maybe *you* would like to write a story about Narnia, or draw your own pictures of it, organise a Narnia party with special food and games, or put on a play based on one of the stories. The idea of this book is to help you do those things. Through it you will find many new ways of enjoying the Chronicles of Narnia and the creations of C. S. Lewis's imagination; but most of all (because it is what he would have wanted) I hope it will encourage you to use your own imagination…

Brian Sibley

Mr Tumnus Mask

White Witch's Ice Recipe

Narnia is a land of glittering icicles. Mr Tumnus tells Lucy that the White Witch makes it always winter. *(You will need grown-up help with this recipe.)*

Coconut Ice
enough for eight people

1 lb granulated sugar
¼ pint of water
butter for greasing tin
4 oz desiccated coconut

1   Put the sugar and water into the pan and heat gently until dissolved.
2   Grease a tin 6″ x 2½″ with some butter.
3   Ask a grown-up to help with this stage. Bring the sugar syrup to the boil, boil rapidly for 3 minutes, then test a drop in glass of cold water. It should form a soft ball; if necessary, continue boiling and re-test. Remove the pan from the heat.
4   Add the desiccated coconut and mix it in thoroughly. Continue to stir mixture well as it cools.
5   When the mixture has become really thick, quickly put it into the tin and smooth the top. Put the tin in a cool place and leave it to cool.
6   When the coconut is cold divide it into fingers.

When Lucy stumbles into Narnia through the wardrobe, she meets a Faun called Mr Tumnus who invites her to his cave for a wonderful tea. You can make a Mr Tumnus mask.

Trace these outlines on to thin card.

and Narnia Recipes

Mr Tumnus's Sugar-Topped Cake

Mr Tumnus invites Lucy for a wonderful tea which includes a sugar-topped cake. This is how you make it.

Sugar-Topped Cake
2 Victoria sponge
sandwich cakes
2 oz butter
4 oz icing sugar
1 lemon
glacé cherry

1 Soften the butter in a bowl and cream it with a wooden spoon until it is quite soft.
2 Sieve the icing sugar. Gradually beat in the icing sugar until it has all been added and the mixture is light and fluffy.
3 Grate the lemon rind and add it to the icing; squeeze the lemon and strain one table-spoon of juice into the mixture.
4 Spread half the icing mixture on to one of the sandwich cakes and put them together.
5 Put the rest of mixture on top of the cake with a palette knife and shape it to look like snow peaks.
6 Top with a cherry.

Colour in the face, hair and horns.
   Cut round the outside edge of the mask. Cut holes for your eyes. Tape a ribbon to the back of each ear or thread through some thin elastic so you can fix the mask round your head.

Mr Tumnus and the White Witch

*S*uddenly Mr Tumnus's brown eyes fill with tears. He tells Lucy he's crying because he has orders from the White Witch that if ever he sees any Daughters of Eve, he must catch them and hand them over to her.

Lucy asks him who the White Witch is. Mr Tumnus tells her, "Why, it is she that has got all Narnia under her thumb. It's she that makes it always winter. Always winter and never Christmas; think of that!"

Draw a picture of the White Witch in a snowy Narnian scene. You can see what kind of crown she wears from the picture on p.17.

The Stone Party

In *The Lion, the Witch and the Wardrobe*, the White Witch is driving through the snow on her sledge on the trail of the Beavers and the children, when she comes upon a merry party, "a squirrel and his wife with their children and two satyrs and a dwarf and an old dog-fox" having a feast.

The evil Witch is so angry when she hears that Father Christmas gave them the good things they are eating that she turns them into stone. C. S. Lewis used to get lots of letters asking what happened to the stone animals and he replied that of course, Aslan turned them back again, although it is not mentioned in the story. If you had been one of the little animals turned to stone, what would it have been like? Write this postcard to a friend explaining what happened.

POSTCARD

NARNIA
XIIM
IR PARA

SCENE · ON · FRONT:
NARNIAN CHRISTMAS PARTY.

Putting on a Narnia Play

If you've ever wished you could be a part of the Chronicles of Narnia then there is one way in which you can be – by putting on a Narnia play. You could write and perform a play based on one of the Narnia stories for a puppet theatre or for a toy theatre (using cut-out figures based on the pictures in the books), or you could make a play for you and your friends to act. This is how to go about it.

The Audience
Putting on a play can be great fun for those who are acting and those who are watching but to do it well you have to plan it carefully. The first thing you will need is an audience, so begin by deciding when and where you are going to put on your play and who you are performing for – maybe your schoolfriends or your family.

Choosing a Play
The next thing is to choose which Narnia story, or part of a story, you want to make into a play. You may find it easier to act out just one or two scenes from a book rather than the whole thing, but you could do quite a few scenes and link them together with someone reading or telling the audience the parts of the story that go between the scenes. This can also help you with any scenes which you think are too difficult to act out.

Try to choose scenes which have lots

of conversation and action in them because they will be more interesting for the audience. You also need to pick episodes that have the right number of characters for however many of you are putting on the play. For example, if there are only two of you, you might do the scene with Lucy and Mr Tumnus; if there are three of you, you could be Eustace, Jill and Puddleglum, or Polly, Digory and Jadis and if there are as many as six of you, you could play Peter, Susan, Lucy, Edmund and Mr and Mrs Beaver.

To make sure your play is a success, you will have to practise it, or as actors call it, 'rehearse'. Begin by deciding if you are going to learn a script or 'improvise' (that means that although you don't have a proper script, you have all read the episode in the book several times and you are agreed between yourselves who is going to say what). Then you rehearse the play until everybody remembers their parts.

You can write out the play, using the words that the characters use in the book, but leaving out all the descriptions and things like 'he said' or 'said Lucy'. This will take time and all the actors will need a copy of the same words. It is much more enjoyable for an audience if you all learn or make up the words rather than read them out of a book. It is also very difficult to move about and act if you are trying to read at the same time.

In this book you will find two play-scripts. *Edmund meets the White Witch* is for two actors and *Prince Caspian Returns to Narnia* is for five actors. You might prefer to choose a scene of your own and write your own script.

Where shall we put on the play?
You probably won't have a real stage, so decide where you are going to put on your play. You could use a room in your home or perform outside in a garden or yard. If you are putting the play on at school, you could use your classroom, the school hall or the playground. Decide where the audience is going to sit, making sure that everyone will be able to see and that you will have enough space to act in. Make sure you decide where the actors are going to be before they come on stage. Perhaps you can set up your stage near a door, or you can hide characters behind chairs or a screen until it is time for them to come on.

You will find useful things around the house to make the set or for props. Two chairs covered in a sheet make the White Witch's sledge, a playhouse or small tent could be Mr Tumnus's or the Beavers' house. Make sure everything is in place before you begin.

Music and Sound Effects
You might like to introduce your play with some suitable music on a tape-

recorder. Or perhaps one of the cast could play Mr Tumnus's tune from this book on the piano or recorder. You could make a tape of sound effects (such as wind, wolves howling, birdsong, the cracking of the Stone Table) either by recording the sound yourselves, or by borrowing a sound effects tape from your local library. Make sure that you record enough effects if you want them to run through a whole scene and be sure to rehearse beforehand so that you bring them in at the right time.

Make-up and costumes?

Don't worry too much about make-up and costumes – what is important is that people believe in the character you are playing. If you want to use some make-up, then you can use face-paints (available in theatrical shops and some department stores) or perhaps you can borrow some grown-up make-up (but make sure you ask first). Don't use too much make-up – just enough to suggest the character

you are playing. You could use white powder and red lipstick for the White Witch, or paint on a black nose and whiskers for the Beavers. You might prefer to make masks: this book explains how to make a Mr Tumnus mask, an Aslan and a Beaver mask.

If you are playing the children, you can wear your school uniforms or your ordinary clothes. If you use a storyteller or narrator, they would look very smart in a dark skirt or trousers and a white shirt with a bow tie. Many of the characters in Narnia are either animals or people in historical costumes, so for them you can be very imaginative. For the kings and queens you can make cut-out crowns from cardboard. This book shows you how to make the White Witch's crown. Perhaps you can borrow some jewellery to decorate your clothes. Dressing-gowns can be used as robes and a raincoat worn across the shoulders and buttoned with the top button will make a cloak. Old sheets and curtains can also be used for cloaks (make sure you ask

first). A nightdress or the jacket of a pair of pyjamas make a tunic if tied with a belt, and if you are acting a scene with characters from Calormen you could wear scarves as turbans or a towel tied round the forehead with a necktie. Swords and daggers can be made from cardboard or wood — don't use anything sharp or pointed. This book explains how to make Peter's shield and how to make some armour.

If you are playing one of the animal characters, then try to find clothes that are roughly the same colour as the animal, such as black or brown. Brown or black balaclavas will help give your face a more animal look, or you can use an old pair of tights with a hole cut out for the face. Useful clothes for animal costumes are cords, col-oured tights, leotards, long socks, gloves or fingerless mittens, woolly pullovers and fur-fabric coats and hats. A dressing-gown cord makes a good tail!

Now everything is ready and it's time to ring up the curtain and on with the show!

The White Witch's Crown

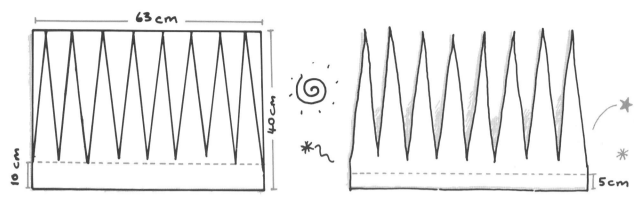

1   Draw the crown on a big piece of stiff card. Make sure the bottom of the spikes are about 10 cm from the bottom of the card.

2   Cut out the crown. It will look like this. Make a fold about 5 cm up from the bottom edge of the card. Press along the fold with the closed blades of your scissors.

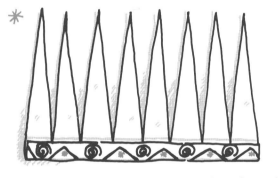

3   Decorate the folded edge by glueing on some braid, fur trimming or sequins; or, if you prefer, paint a design on it.

4   Bend the card round into a crown shape and glue the edges together.

5   Holding each spike of the crown from the inside, pull the closed scissors' blade along the outside edge. This will make the spikes curl outwards.

Edmund Meets the White Witch

(The White Witch is sitting on her sledge. Beside her, unseen by the audience, she has a drink and a box of Turkish Delight.)

WITCH	Stop! Stop the sledge! (*To Edmund*) And what, pray, are you?
EDMUND	I'm – I'm – my name's Edmund…
WITCH	Is that how you address a Queen?
EDMUND	I beg your pardon, Your Majesty, I didn't know.
WITCH	Not know the Queen of Narnia? Ha! You shall know us better hereafter. But I repeat – what are you?
EDMUND	Please, Your Majesty, I don't know what you mean. I'm at school – at least I was – it's the holidays now.
WITCH	But what *are* you? Are you an overgrown dwarf that has cut off its beard?

PLAY

Edmund meets the White Witch

EDMUND	No, Your Majesty. I never had a beard, I'm a boy.
WITCH	A boy! Do you mean you are a Son of Adam?
EDMUND	I don't understand, Your Majesty…
WITCH	Well, I see you are an idiot whatever else you may be! Answer me, once and for all, or I shall lose my patience. Are you human?
EDMUND	Yes, Your Majesty.
WITCH	And how, pray, did you come to enter my dominions?
EDMUND	Please, Your Majesty, I came in through a wardrobe.
WITCH	A wardrobe? What do you mean?
EDMUND	I – I opened a door and just found myself here, Your Majesty.
WITCH	(*To herself*) Ha! A door. A door from the World of Men! I have heard of such things. This may wreck all. But he is only one, and he is easily dealt with. (*To Edmund*) My poor child, how cold you look! Come and sit with me here on the sledge and we will talk.
	(*Edmund climbs on to the sledge, facing the Witch.*)
WITCH	Perhaps something hot to drink? Would you like that?
EDMUND	(*Shivering*) Yes, please, Your Majesty.
	(*The Witch produces a glass and gives it to Edmund, who drinks.*)
WITCH	It is dull, Son of Adam, to drink without eating. What would you like best to eat?
EDMUND	Turkish Delight, please, Your Majesty.
	(*The Witch hands Edmund the box of Turkish Delight which he opens and begins to eat.*)

PLAY
Edmund meets the White Witch

WITCH   Is this your first visit to Narnia?

EDMUND   It's the first time *I've* been here, but my sister has been here before.

WITCH   Your sister?

EDMUND   Lucy. She got in the other day and met a Faun who took her home for tea.

WITCH   Did you say a Faun? What was his name?

EDMUND   Mr Tumnus, she said his name was. I didn't believe her when she told us.

WITCH   Us?

EDMUND   My brother and sister and I.

WITCH   There are four of you?

EDMUND   That's right: Peter, Susan, Lucy and I. Why do you ask?

WITCH   Two Sons of Adam and Two Daughters of Eve? Neither more nor less?

EDMUND   Yes, I just told you that.

WITCH   Son of Adam, I should so much like to see your brother and your two sisters. Will you bring them to see me?

EDMUND   (*Eating the last of the Turkish Delight*) I'll try.

PLAY

....

Edmund meets the White Witch

WITCH   Because, if you did come again – bringing them with you of course – I'd be able to give you some more Turkish Delight. I can't do it now, the magic will only work once. In my own house it would be another matter.

EDMUND   Why can't we go to your house now?

WITCH   It is a lovely place, my house. I am sure you would like it. There are whole rooms full of Turkish Delight, and what's more, I have no children of my own. I want a nice boy whom I could bring up as a prince and who would be King of Narnia when I am gone. While he was prince he would wear a gold crown and eat Turkish Delight all day long; and you are much the cleverest and handsomest young man I've ever met. I think I would like to make you the prince – someday, when you bring the others to visit me.

EDMUND   Why not now?

WITCH   Oh, but if I took you there now, I shouldn't see your brother and your sisters. I very much want to know your charming relations. You are to be the prince and – later on – the King; that is understood. But you must have courtiers and nobles. I will make your brother a Duke and your sisters Duchesses.

EDMUND   There's nothing special about *them*; and, anyway, I could always bring them some other time.

WITCH   Ah, but when you were in my house, you might forget all about them. You would be enjoying yourself so much that you wouldn't want the bother of going to fetch them. No. You must go back to your own country now and come to me another day, *with them*, you understand. It is no good coming without them.

PLAY

Edmund meets the White Witch

EDMUND   But I don't even know the way back to my own country.

WITCH   That's easy. Do you see that lamp? Straight on, beyond that, is the way to the World of Men. And now look the other way, and tell me if you can see two little hills rising above the trees.

EDMUND   I think I can.

WITCH   Well, my house is between those two hills. But remember – you must bring the others with you. I might have to be very angry with you if you came alone.

EDMUND   I'll do my best.

(Edmund gets out of the sledge.)

WITCH   And by the way, you needn't tell them about me. It would be fun to keep it a surprise between us two, wouldn't it? Just bring them along to the two hills – a clever boy like you will easily think of some excuse for doing that – and when you come to my house you could just say "Let's see who lives here", or something like that. I am sure that would be best. If your sister has met one of the Fauns, she may have heard strange stories about me – nasty stories that might make her afraid to come to me. Fauns will say anything.

EDMUND   Please, please, please couldn't I have just one piece of Turkish Delight to eat on the way home?

WITCH   No, no, you must wait till next time! Don't forget. Come soon!

Aslan Mask

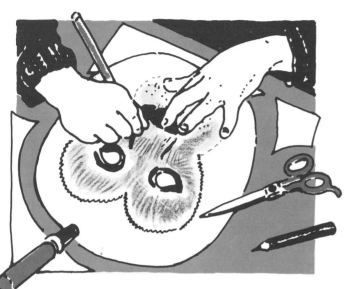

1   Trace Aslan's head, from the opposite page, on to stiff card. Cut it out and colour in his face within the zig-zag line.

2   Cut out the eyes and cut along the dotted line round the muzzle.

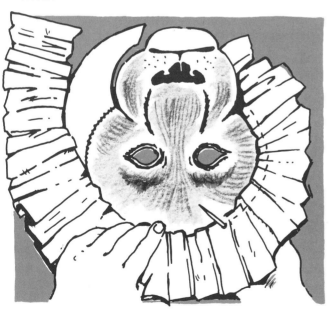

3   To make the mane, fold a long strip of orange crêpe paper into pleats and sew it round Aslan's face along the zigzag line. Snip the outer edges to make the mane look shaggy.

4   Tape or staple the mask together at the places marked with the large dots. This will make the nose and mouth part of the mask stick forwards.
Attach ribbons or elastic on either side.

cut out

cut out

cut along this dotted line

Castles of Narnia

1

2

There are many wonderful castles and palaces in Narnia; some of them are dark and mysterious, others are light and beautiful – nearly all are magical. Here are pictures of six. Do you know which they are? Answers p.62.

3

4

5

6

Spot the Differences

In *The Magician's Nephew*, Polly and Digory explore a ruined palace and find a room full of people, all seated and all perfectly still…"They were like the most wonderful wax-works you ever saw".

These are some of the people they saw. Look carefully at the two pictures and see if you can spot fifteen differences between them. Answers p.62.

1   2   3   4   5   6   7   8

1   2   3   4   5   6   7   8

Trufflehunter's Puzzle

Using the letters in Trufflehunter's name, see how many of the words and names across you know. Answers p.62.

1 The good dwarf in *Prince Caspian*.
2 The mouse who sails with the *Dawn Treader*.
3 The land ruled over by the Green Witch in *The Silver Chair*.

8 The female talking horse in *The Horse and His Boy*.
9 The creature called Jewel in *The Last Battle*.
10 The land ruled by Aslan.

1 T ....
2 R ....
3 U ....
4 F ....
5 F ....
6 L ....
7 E ....
8 H ....
9 U ....
10 N ....
11 T ....
12 E ....
13 R ....

4 The flying horse in *The Magician's Nephew*.
5 The eagle in *The Last Battle*.
6 Uncle Andrew's sister in *The Magician's Nephew*.
7 The boy who is given Turkish Delight by the White Witch.

11 The first person Lucy meets in Narnia.
12 The boy who is turned into a dragon in *The Voyage of the Dawn Treader*.
13 The lost Prince found by Jill and Eustace in *The Silver Chair*.

Design Some Narnian Stamps

What would you draw on a Narnian postage stamp? You could put a tiny lion's head in one corner and think up special designs to commemorate such events as the defeat of the White Witch; the launching of the *Dawn Treader*; the Coronation of the Pevensie children or of King Caspian. Other stamps could show places of interest like the lamp-post, the Stone Table or the Castle at Cair Paravel; heroes of Narnia (such as Reepicheep the mouse or Roonwit the centaur) or weird and wonderful Narnian characters like sprites and satyrs, dwarfs, and dryads, giants and unicorns.

Narnia Party Invitations

Do your friends enjoy *The Chronicles of Narnia* as much as you do? Why not have a Narnia party – either to celebrate a birthday or just because it would be fun to have a party? You could ask your friends to dress up as Narnia characters, make Narnian food and play games with Narnian themes. Have a good party!

First things first:
Draw your own invitations on plain postcards.
Look through your Narnia books for picture ideas.

Please come to a Narnia party on Saturday, March 3 from 3 – 6.30 pm

P.S. Please dress up as a Narnia character

Come to a Narnian banquet

we're off to a Narnia Party!

Narnia Party Food

The Centaurs' Oaten Cakes

Caspian meets the great Centaur Glenstorm and his three sons who provide oaten cakes as they journey to the Dancing Lawn

Oaten split cakes
makes 8 oaten cakes

6 oz plain flour
1 teaspoon of bicarbonate of soda
2 teaspoons of cream of tartar
salt
2 oz medium oatmeal
2 oz butter
5 fl oz milk

1   Switch the oven to gas mark 7/ 200°C/400°F to preheat and grease an oven sheet.
2   Sift the flour, bicarbonate of soda, cream of tartar and ½ teaspoon of salt together into a bowl and stir in the oatmeal.
3   Cut the butter into small pieces and rub into the dry ingredients, then mix in just enough milk to make a soft dough.
4   Knead lightly then flatten to a thickness of 1 inch and cut 8 rounds from this with a fluted cutter.
5   Bake the oaten cakes for 10 minutes and then turn off the oven and leave for another 5 minutes.
6   Cool on a wire rack.
7   Split the cakes by pulling apart with your fingers. Spoon thick cream and honey or wild fruits such as strawberries onto each half.

Cair Paravel Apples

With only a bag of sandwiches each to keep them going, Edmund, Lucy, Susan and Peter are pleased to find a tree laden with large yellowish apples in the orchard at Cair Paravel.

Roast Apples
One apple per person
Brown sugar
Butter
Chilled cream

1   Wash and core the apples. Make a skin-deep cut right round the 'equator' of each apple so the skin will lift as the apple fluffs up and it won't burst.
2   Allow one apple per person and crowd them in a roasting tin.
3   Fill the centres where the cores used to be with brown sugar.
4   Put a good flake of butter on the top of each apple and pour 2-3 tablespoons of cold water into the pan.
5   Cook for 45 minutes in a moderate oven. Serve piping hot, with the syrup from the pan spooned over the apples and chilled cream to cool them down.

Narnia Party Food

Edmund's Turkish Delight

When Edmund asks the White Witch for Turkish Delight he finds it so delicious that he eats the whole box. *(You will need a grown-up to help you with this recipe.)*

Turkish Delight
makes about 16 chunky pieces

1½ lb of sugar
1 lemon
1 orange
¼ pint of water
3 oz cornflour
1 oz gelatine
icing sugar

1   Put the sugar, the pared rind and juice of the lemon and orange and ¼ pint of water into a copper pan.
2   Make sure you have grown-up help for this next stage. Bring the contents of the pan slowly to the boil, making sure the sugar is dissolved before boiling point is reached. Test with a cookery thermometer and boil to 110° C (230° F).
3   Stir the cornflour into a little water and add it to the syrup.
4   Have ready the gelatine softened in a little water, add it to the pan and boil until clear, stirring occasionally.
5   Strain the mixture into tins about 1 inch deep and leave until the following day.
6   Cut into squares and roll in icing sugar.

Mrs Beaver's Marmalade Roll

Tea with Mr and Mrs Beaver is a treat. Lucy, Peter and Susan are given creamy milk to drink and deep yellow butter to eat with potatoes and freshwater fish. When they finish the fish Mrs Beaver quite unexpectedly gives them a great and gloriously sticky marmalade roll…

Marmalade Roll
for eight people

1 packet of ginger biscuits
marmalade
whipped double cream
crystallised orange segments
preserved stem ginger

1   Spread the biscuits with marmalade and clamp them all together in one long sandwich shaped like a log.
2   Cover the ginger and marmalade roll with whipped double cream and decorate with crystallised orange segments and the ginger.

Narnia Party Food

Pattertwig's Fruit and Nut Munch

In *Prince Caspian*, Caspian meets a magnificent red squirrel, Pattertwig, who presents him with a nut from his hoard. You can make this delicious fruit and nut munch.

Fruit and Nut Munch
makes enough to fill a large bowl

12 oz dried apricots (chopped)
12 oz prunes – stoned and chopped
6 oz dried figs – chopped
3 oz banana flakes
6 oz unsalted cashew nuts
3 oz pumpkin seeds
3 oz sunflower seeds
3 oz natural peanuts

1   Mix the fruits together.
2   Lightly toast the nuts and seeds under the grill for 3-4 minutes. Add to the fruit mixture and stir well.
3   Cool completely and store the munch in an airtight container.
4   Serve in a big party bowl.

The White Witch's Snow Fondants

In Narnia it is always winter.

Fondants
makes about 24 fondants

8 oz icing sugar
1 egg white
¼ teaspoon peppermint essence
1 teaspoon coffee essence
a few nuts

1   Sieve the icing sugar on to clean greaseproof paper.
2   Whip the egg white with a fork until it is light and frothy, then gradually work in the icing sugar. When the fondant mixture is sufficiently stiff, use your hands to work in the rest of the icing sugar.
3   Put half of the mixture on a sugared surface, add peppermint essence to taste and knead; add more sugar if needed.
4   When the mixture is firm and dry, roll to ¼ inch thickness and cut into rounds with a 1 inch cutter.
5   Carefully lift the creams on to a tray lined with greaseproof paper, and leave in a cool place to dry.
6   Flavour the rest of the fondant mixture with coffee essence, roll and cut in rounds as before. Decorate with nuts.
7   When all the creams are quite dry, remove them from the tray and put them into paper sweet cases.

Maugrim's Awake!

The courtyard of the White Witch's castle in *The Lion, the Witch and the Wardrobe* is full of Narnians who have been turned to stone.

To play Maugrim's Awake, one person is chosen to be Maugrim the Wolf (or Fenris Ulf as he is also known), Chief of the White Witch's Secret Police. Everyone else must decide which Narnian character to be – perhaps a satyr, a bear, a fox, a centaur, a winged horse, a dragon, or giant – turned to stone by the Witch's magic. Whenever Maugrim (Fenris Ulf) turns his back on the statues to go to sleep, they can move about, but the moment Maugrim wakes up and turns round, the statues must stand absolutely still, whatever they are doing. If Maugrim sees anyone move, they are out. When you are out you are allowed to help the other statues by shouting "Maugrim's awake!" the moment you see him turn round. The last statue to be left in plays Maugrim in the next game.

Jadis's Apple Game

In *The Magician's Nephew*, Jadis tempts Digory to eat an apple from the enchanted garden. "Eat it, Boy, eat it," she tells him, "and you will live for ever", but Digory refuses to eat. Here's a game that involves eating apples – or trying to!

Set up two chairs, several feet apart, with their backs facing one another and place a long piece of wood or a broomstick across the gap. Tie some apples on to pieces of string and hang them from the stick so they can swing freely between the two chairs. (Have these things ready before the party begins.) Those playing the game have to kneel down in front of one of the apples and try to bite it without using their hands. The winner is the one who eats the most apple – but it is not as easy as it sounds!

The Invisible Dufflepud Game

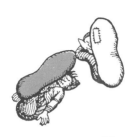

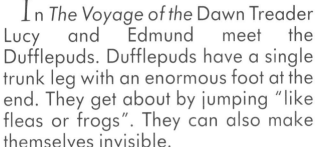

In *The Voyage of the* Dawn Treader Lucy and Edmund meet the Dufflepuds. Dufflepuds have a single trunk leg with an enormous foot at the end. They get about by jumping "like fleas or frogs". They can also make themselves invisible.

To play the Invisible Dufflepud Game a girl is chosen to be Lucy and a boy to be Edmund. They are then blindfolded so that the Dufflepud players are invisible to them. Everyone else is a Dufflepud and must tie their ankles together (use a handkerchief or an old tie) so that they can only hop about. Lucy and Edmund must then catch as many Dufflepuds as possible. The Dufflepuds must keep hopping about, talking as they hop (Dufflepuds always talk a lot). When a Dufflepud is caught, they are out. The last girl to be caught is Lucy in the next game, and the last boy to be caught, Edmund.

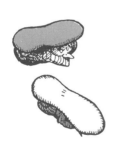

You can also have Dufflepud races, but make sure you have them where the Dufflepuds won't hurt themselves if they fall over – they probably will!

Reepicheep's Tail

In *Prince Caspian*, the proud little Reepicheep loses his tail in battle. He seeks Aslan's help and the great lion asks the mouse why he needs a tail.

Reepicheep explains," I can eat and sleep and die for my king without one. But a tail is the honour and glory of a mouse."

You can play putting the tail on Reepicheep as a party game. Trace this drawing of him on to some paper and pin it on a wall.

Put a drawing pin in one end of a length of string. Take it in turns with your friends to be blindfolded and try to pin this tail in the right place on Reepicheep. It's trickier than you might think!

Who Am I?

Prince Corin

Eustace as a dragon

Doctor Cornelius

Lucy

In *The Voyage of the Dawn Treader*, Eustace is turned into a dragon. The others draw their swords and are preparing to fight when Lucy realises that the dragon is crying.

Eventually, after many questions they guess that it is Eustace. To play Who Am I, one person chooses to be a character in Narnia such as Aslan the lion or Reepicheep the mouse or the White Witch. The others can ask up to twenty questions to find out who it is. They can ask all sorts of questions, such as "how big are you?" "do you like Turkish Delight?" "do you live underground?", and so on. The first player to guess who the person is becomes the next person to be a Narnian character.

Puddleglum

Aravis

Reepicheep

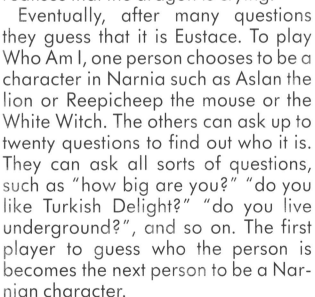

Giant Wimbleweather

Mr Tumnus's Parcels

Do you remember Lucy's first meeting with Mr Tumnus? He is hurrying through the snowy wood carrying an umbrella and several brown paper parcels. "What with the parcels and the snow it looked just as if he had been doing his Christmas shopping...And when he saw Lucy he gave such a start of surprise that he dropped all his parcels".

To play Mr Tumnus's Parcels you will need at least twenty parcels. You can make these out of empty cereal boxes and washing powder or tissue boxes. They will look more attractive if you cover them in old Christmas wrapping paper or paint them bright colours.

Divide the players into two teams and line them up at one end of the room. Each team chooses one person to be their Mr Tumnus. The Mr Tumnuses stand at the other end of the room facing their teams. When the game starts, each team member in turn, and as quickly as possible, picks up a parcel, runs to hand it to Mr Tumnus and runs back. This continues until all the parcels have been used up. Mr Tumnus must then run to the team carrying all the parcels and trying not to drop them. The winner of each round is the team who is back first.

Scoring

The first team home wins six points. Each team also wins one point for each parcel not dropped. If no parcels were dropped, a bonus of four points is given. Keep playing until everyone has had a turn as Mr Tumnus, then add up the total number of points for each team to see who has won.

Mr Tumnus's Tune

When Lucy has tea with Mr Tumnus, the faun plays for her on "a strange little flute that looked as if it were made of straw…And the tune he played made Lucy want to cry and laugh and dance and sleep all at the same time".

Here is some music for Mr Tumnus's tune, that you can play on the recorder. This tune could be played at your

Narnia party or used as part of a Narnia play.

37

The Children's Coronation

In *The Lion, The Witch and The Wardrobe*, the four children, are crowned kings and queens of Narnia by Aslan in the great hall of Cair Paravel.

Draw portraits of the new kings and queens seated on their thrones, with crowns on their heads and sceptres in their hands, in this frame below.

After the Coronation

After the coronation, there is a great feast, with revelry and dancing. If you had been preparing the banquet, what food would you have prepared for it? Write down the sumptuous menu you would have provided.

dinner	puddings	drinks

The Laws of Narnia

Once Peter, Susan, Lucy and Edmund become kings and queens of Narnia, they govern it well. "They made good laws and kept the peace and saved good trees from being unnecessarily cut down and liberated young dwarfs and satyrs from being sent to school…" If you were ruler of Narnia, what five good laws would you make? Write them down on the scroll below.

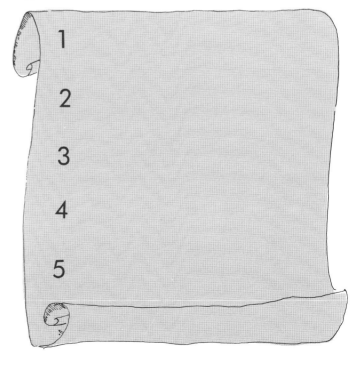

1

2

3

4

5

The Dawn Treader Word Search

Can you find eleven words connected with *The Voyage of the Dawn Treader* in the wordsquare below? The picture clues will help you. Answers p.62.

D	U	F	F	L	E	P	U	D	I	N	O
S	A	U	P	S	L	A	N	P	S	P	E
E	R	W	N	A	I	P	S	A	C	E	R
R	L	T	N	W	I	O	L	E	O	E	D
A	E	U	S	T	A	C	E	D	I	H	A
M	F	F	C	G	R	A	U	M	R	C	W
A	N	L	E	Y	L	E	S	U	E	I	T
N	O	G	A	R	D	B	A	N	E	P	O
D	P	N	A	I	N	I	R	D	P	E	R
U	A	L	U	M	P	A	S	U	E	E	F
S	E	A	P	E	O	P	L	E	L	R	T

and Picture to Colour in

A Narnia Quiz

*T*est your knowledge of Narnia with these questions – or try them out on your friends. Answers p.62.

1. What does Lucy find in the wardrobe before she discovers the way in to Narnia?
2. What animal does Shasta meet among the tombs in *The Horse and His Boy*?
3. What does the lamb turn into at the end of *The Voyage of the Dawn Treader*?
4. What gift does Father Christmas give Mrs Beaver?
5. What vehicle does Queen Jadis steal when she visits London in *The Magician's Nephew*?
6. What does the White Witch use to kill Aslan?
7. What kind of creature is Trufflehunter?
8. How do the children in *The Voyage of the* Dawn Treader enter Narnia?
9. How does Shift the ape make people believe that Puzzle the donkey is really Aslan in *The Last Battle*?
10. What bird leads the four children to Mr Beaver in *The Lion, the Witch and the Wardrobe*?
11. In *The Silver Chair*, who lives in a wigwam on the marshes?
12. To which two characters does Lucy give a handkerchief in *The Lion, the Witch and the Wardrobe*?
13. In *The Horse and His Boy*, who lives with Arsheesh the fisherman?
14. What is Fledge's name before Aslan gives him wings in *The Magician's Nephew*?
15. What kind of animal is Maugrim (Fenris Ulf), Captain of the White Witch's Secret Police in *The Lion, the Witch and the Wardrobe*?
16. Of what ship is Drinian the captain?
17. Who calls herself "Queen of Narnia"?
18. On what animals does Uncle Andrew experiment in *The Magician's Nephew*?
19. What is the name of the terrible bird-headed creature in *The Last Battle*?
20. Which king of Narnia sails away in a ship at the beginning of *The Silver Chair*?

The Magic Book

In *The Voyage of the* Dawn Treader Lucy finds the Magic Book of Spells to cure all kinds of things — warts, toothache, cramp, taking a swarm of bees and invisibleness. Can you write a spell of your own on this page from the Magic Book?

Over the Hills to Cair Paravel

The castle of Cair Paravel stands by the sea on the eastern shore of Narnia. Can you help Mr Tumnus find his way there through the hills and forests? Answers p.63.

Scrambled Narnian Names

Here are some places in Narnia but the front halves of the names don't go with the back halves. Can you sort them out? Answers p.63.

CALOR-MOOR ....   LANTERN-HOW ....
AN-MA ....   ARCHEN-MEN ....
GLASS-LAND ....   ETTINS-BAAN ....
ASLAN'S WASTE ....   HAR-WATER ....
TASH-FANG ....   GAL-VARD ....

How well do you know the names of the characters in Narnia? Here are some that have had their letters muddled up. See how many you can untangle.
Answers p.63.

SALAN ....   TOINWRO ....
PECEHIPERE ....   SPACINA ....
HASAST ....   YOGRID ....
PRUNKTIM ....   NARUDAM ....

What's In A Name?

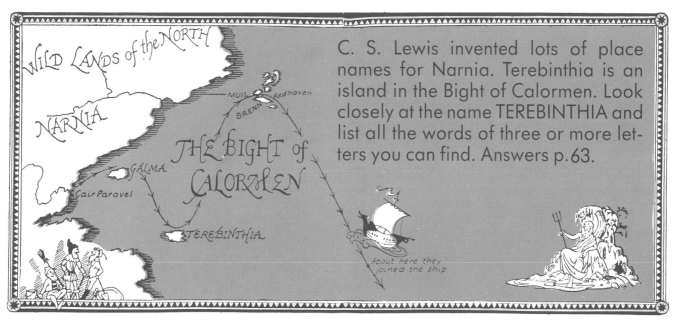

C. S. Lewis invented lots of place names for Narnia. Terebinthia is an island in the Bight of Calormen. Look closely at the name TEREBINTHIA and list all the words of three or more letters you can find. Answers p.63.

MAKE

Beaver Mask

In *The Lion, the Witch and the Wardrobe*, Mr and Mrs Beaver look after Peter, Susan and Lucy and take them to the Stone Table to meet Aslan.

If you want to dress up as Mr or Mrs Beaver for a Narnia party or play, here is an easy way to make a Beaver mask as part of your costume.

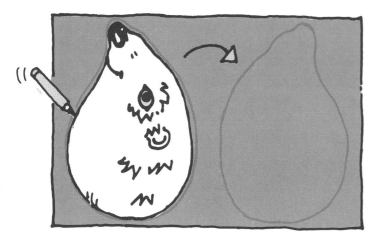

1   Trace the template on the opposite page twice on to card and cut out two mask faces.

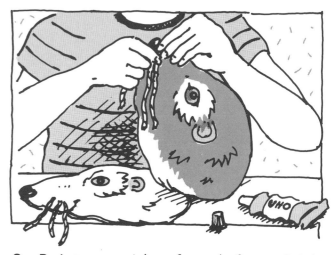

2   Paint one side of each face. Stick on some short lengths of black wool for the whiskers.

3   Cut two strips of card – one long enough to fit over the top of your head and the other long enough to fit round the back of your head. Paint them brown.

4   Tape both strips to the inside of the faces – one at the back and the other just in front of the ears. Staple the noses together. Try on the mask and adjust the fit, if necessary.

Shadows from Narnia

1 _____

Here are silhouettes of some Narnian animals. Can you identify what they are? Answers p.63.

2 _____

3 _____

4 _____

5 _____

6 _____

A Day with the Beavers

In *The Lion, the Witch and the Wardrobe*, Mr and Mrs Beaver welcome Peter, Susan, Edmund and Lucy into their snug little house and give them a hearty dinner.

Have you ever seen a room like this before? "Instead of beds there were bunks like on board ship built into the wall. And there were hams and strings of onions hanging from the roof."

Look carefully at the picture and see if you can see at least twelve things beginning with the letter S. Answers p.63.

Prince Caspian Returns to Old Narnia

Characters:
Narrator
Prince Caspian

Nikabrik (a dwarf)
Trumpkin (a dwarf)
Trufflehunter (a badger)

(On the right hand side of the stage Prince Caspian is lying on his back on a table or on three chairs with a pillow under his head and a rug over him. He appears to be asleep. Trufflehunter, Nikabrik and Trumpkin are huddled together on the other side of the stage deep in discussion.)

NARRATOR

Prince Caspian has escaped from his wicked uncle King Miraz and is looking for the Old Narnians he has heard about in stories and legends. Caught in a storm, his horse bolts and Caspian hits his head on a tree. He is found by three friends…

TRUFFLEHUNTER

Before it wakes up, we must decide what to do with it.

NIKABRIK

Kill it! We can't let it live. It would betray us.

(Caspian opens his eyes, but does not move.)

TRUMPKIN

We ought to have killed it at once, or else let it alone. We can't kill it now. Not after we've taken it in and bandaged its head and all. It would be murdering a guest.

CASPIAN

Gentlemen, whatever you do to me, I hope you will be kind to my poor horse.

(The others turn and look at him.)

TRUFFLEHUNTER

Your horse had taken flight long before we found you.

NIKABRIK	Now don't let it talk you round with its pretty words. I still say…
TRUMPKIN	(*Interrupting*) Horns and halibuts! Of course we're not going to murder it. For shame, Nikabrik. What do you say, Trufflehunter? What shall we do with it?
TRUFFLEHUNTER	What I say, Trumpkin, is I shall give it a drink.
	(*Trufflehunter crosses to where Caspian is lying with a mug and props the Prince up so he can drink. Caspian looks startled on seeing that Trufflehunter is a badger.*)

CASPIAN	You're a badger!
TRUFFLEHUNTER	Certainly I am.
CASPIAN	But you can talk!
TRUFFLEHUNTER	Of course I can talk.
	(*Trumpkin and Nikabrik join Trufflehunter at Caspian's side.*)
CASPIAN	And who are your friends?
TRUMPKIN	Picks and pitchforks! We're Dwarfs, of course!
CASPIAN	Then I've found who I was looking for.

PLAY

Prince Caspian Returns to Old Narnia

NIKABRIK	And who might that be?
CASPIAN	The Old Narnians.
NARRATOR	After a few days, Caspian is well enough to sit up and talk. But he finds that he is still not out of danger.
	(Caspian is sitting on one of the chairs and Trufflehunter is sitting beside him. Trumpkin is standing stage right looking at the Prince, while Nikabrik paces to and fro behind them.)
NIKABRIK	We still have to decide what to do with this Human. You two think you've done it a great kindness by not letting me kill it. But I suppose now we will have to keep it a prisoner for life. I'm certainly not going to let it go alive – to go back to its own kind and betray us all!
TRUMPKIN	Bulbs and bolsters, Nikabrik! It isn't the creature's fault that it bashed its head against a tree outside our hole. And I don't think it looks like a traitor.
CASPIAN	You haven't yet found out whether I want to go back. Well, I don't. I want to stay with you – if you'll let me. I've been looking for people like you all my life.
TRUFFLEHUNTER	*(Smiling)* Have you really?
NIKABRIK	That's a likely story! You're a Human, aren't you? Of course you want to go back to your own kind.
CASPIAN	Well, even if I did, I couldn't. I was flying for my life when I had my accident. King Miraz wants to kill me. If you'd killed me, you'd have done the very thing to please him.
TRUFFLEHUNTER	Well now, you don't say so!
TRUMPKIN	What have you been doing, Human, to fall foul of Miraz at your age?

(Caspian gets up.)

CASPIAN He's my uncle…

(Nikabrik draws a dagger.)

NIKABRIK There you are! Not only a Human, but close kin and heir to our greatest enemy! Are you still mad enough to let this creature live?

(Nikabrik attacks Caspian but Trufflehunter jumps up and stands in front of the Prince and Trumpkin grabs Nikabrik and snatches the dagger from his hand.)

TRUMPKIN Once and for all, Nikabrik, will you contain yourself, or must Trufflehunter and I sit on your head?

(Nikabrik sulkily crosses to the other side of the stage.)

NIKABRIK All right, all right!

TRUFFLEHUNTER Go on with your story.

CASPIAN Ever since I was a little boy, I've heard about Old Narnia and the Dwarfs and the Talking Beasts. My old Nurse used to tell me stories about them and I always wanted to believe in them. Then one day my Tutor told me they were true – and he told me that he knew they were true because he was half-dwarf. So I ran away to look for the Old Narnians myself.

Prince Caspian Returns to Old Narnia

TRUMPKIN	This is the queerest thing I ever heard.
NIKABRIK	I don't like it. I didn't know there were stories about us still told among the Humans. The less they know about us the better! You mark my words, no good will come of it!
TRUFFLEHUNTER	Don't go on about things you don't understand, Nikabrik. You Dwarfs are as forgetful and changeable as the Humans themselves. I'm a beast, I am, and a Badger what's more. We don't change. We hold on. I say great good will come of it. This is the true King of Narnia we've got here: a true King, coming back to true Narnia. And we beasts remember, even if Dwarfs forget, that Narnia was never right except when a son of Adam was king.
TRUMPKIN	Whistles and whirligigs, Trufflehunter! You don't mean you want to give the country to Humans?
TRUFFLEHUNTER	I said nothing about that. It's not Men's country (who should know that better than me?) but it's a country for a man to be king of. We badgers have long enough memories to know that. Why, bless us all, wasn't the High King Peter a Man?
NIKABRIK	*(Turning angrily away)* You make me sick, Badger.
TRUMPKIN	Do you really believe all those old stories?
TRUFFLEHUNTER	I tell you, we don't change, we beasts. We don't forget. I believe in the High King Peter and the rest that reigned at Cair Paravel, as firmly as I believe in Aslan himself!
NIKABRIK	Pah! As firmly as that!
TRUMPKIN	Who believes in Aslan nowadays?

PLAY

Prince Caspian Returns to Old Narnia

CASPIAN	I do! And if I hadn't believed in him before, I would now. Back there among the Humans the people who laughed at Aslan would have laughed at stories about Talking Beasts and Dwarfs. Sometimes I did wonder if there really was such a person as Aslan: but then sometimes I wondered if there really were people like you. Yet there you are.
TRUFFLEHUNTER	That's right, King Caspian. Here we are! And as long as you will be true to Old Narnia you shall be my King! *(To the Dwarfs)* What do you say?
NIKABRIK	I say no good will come of this at all!
CASPIAN	And what about you, Trumpkin?
TRUMPKIN	I agree with Trufflehunter. You shall be my King too.
TRUFFLEHUNTER	Then that's settled! Long life to you, King Caspian! Long life to Your Majesty!
NARRATOR	And that is how Prince Caspian returned to his true people and became King of Old Narnia.

Cruels and Hags

The White Witch in *The Lion, the Witch and the Wardrobe* has an army of terrible creatures. Here are some of their names: "Cruels and Hags and Incubuses, Wraiths, Horrors, Efreets, Sprites, Orknies, Wooses and Ettins."

Make a picture of what they might look like – some might be ghosts or monsters, others might be creatures with horrible fangs and claws.

Walking Trees and Stone Statues

Trees in Narnia are very special. In *The Magician's Nephew* Aslan sings a creation song and then calls his new world to life: "Narnia, Narnia, Narnia, awake. Love. Think. Speak. Be walking trees. Be talking beasts. Be divine waters." When the White Witch is Queen of Narnia in *The Lion, The Witch and the Wardrobe*, Mr Tumnus warns Lucy, "The whole world is full of *her* spies. Even some of the trees are on her side."

See if you can find some pieces of dead wood that you can make into Narnian trees. You can glue on sequins or buttons for eyes or paint them.

When Edmund goes to the White Witch's castle, he finds a courtyard full of stone statues. There are "stone satyrs and stone wolves and bears and foxes and cat-a-mountains of stone. There were lovely stone shapes that looked like women, but were really the spirits of trees. There was a great shape of a centaur and a winged horse and a long lithe creature that Edmund took to be a dragon."

See if you can find some stones that look as if they might once have been a Narnian creature. Paint them and stick on details that make them look more realistic.

Peter's Shield

When Father Christmas visits Narnia, he gives Peter a sword and also a shield "the colour of silver, and across it there ramped a red lion, as bright as a ripe strawberry at the moment when you pick it".

If you would like to make a shield like Peter's, this is how to do it. Cut a piece of stiff card into a shield shape, big enough to fit on the lion shape on the opposite page. It will need to be at least 27cm along the top and 33cm in length. Trace the lion on to the shield and colour it in. Tape two strips of card on to the back of the shield, big enough to fit your arm through.

The lion on Peter's shield represents Aslan and is probably Peter's coat-of-arms. You can design coats-of-arms for your favourite characters using something associated with them: for example, Edmund's shield could have a sword breaking a magic wand; Caspian's could have a picture of the *Dawn Treader* and Eustace's might have a dragon on it.

tape

A Narnian Breastplate

Many of the characters in Narnia wear armour when they go into battle and even the children from our world have to wear it when they are forced to fight against the enemies of Aslan. C. S. Lewis was fascinated by the idea of knights ever since he read about them in books when he was a boy. He said, many years later, that he had always been rather disappointed that he had never owned a suit of armour of his own.

Here is how you can make a simple breastplate out of card. You could paint it or decorate it with silver foil or sticky shapes.

1 Cut two pieces of card about 38 cm x 25 cm into a breastplate shape like the one shown here. Paint or decorate them how you like.

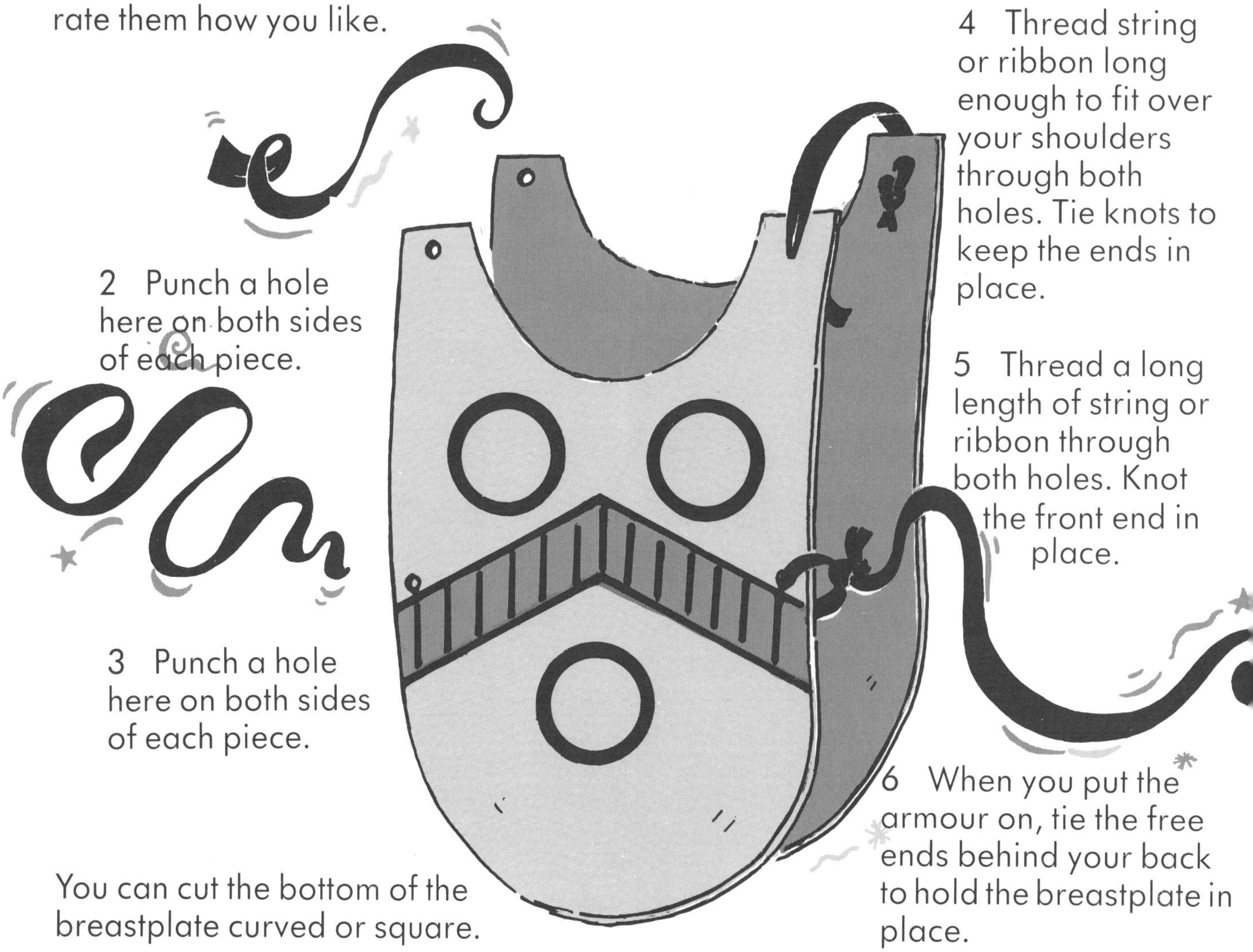

2 Punch a hole here on both sides of each piece.

3 Punch a hole here on both sides of each piece.

You can cut the bottom of the breastplate curved or square.

4 Thread string or ribbon long enough to fit over your shoulders through both holes. Tie knots to keep the ends in place.

5 Thread a long length of string or ribbon through both holes. Knot the front end in place.

6 When you put the armour on, tie the free ends behind your back to hold the breastplate in place.

Back to the Lamp-Post

Beyond the lamp-post in Narnia is the way to the World of Men. Can you help the four children find their way through the woods back to the lamp-post? Beware, there are many false trails and leads.

Answers

Castles of Narnia

1. Anvard, home of King Lune
2. The White Witch's Castle
3. The Palace of the Tisroc in Tashbaan
4. Cair Paravel, home of the kings and queens of Narnia
5. The House of Harfang, home of the Gentle Giants
6. The Magician's House

Spot the differences

In the bottom picture:
Figure 1 has lost 1 her necklace and 2 her throne.
Figure 2 has got 3 a bobble on his crown and 4 his medallion has changed shape.
Figure 3 has 5 acquired a moustache and 6 has a shoe peeping out from under his robes.
Figure 4 has 7 got a bracelet on her right arm and 8 a point on her crown.
Figure 5 has 9 an extra feather in his crown.
Figure 6 has 10 a dangling ear-ring and 11 a veil
Figure 7 has 12 an extra heart-shaped necklace and 13 different jewels on her crown.
Figure 8 has 14 grown a beard and 15 lost his brooch.

Trufflehunter's Puzzle

1. Trumpkin	8. Hwin
2. Reepicheep	9. Unicorn
3. Underland	10. Narnia
4. Fledge	11. Tumnus
5. Farsight	12. Eustace
6. Letty	13. Rilian
7. Edmund	

The Dawn Treader Word Search

Dawn Treader	Reepicheep	Eustace
Dufflepud	Ramandu	Lucy
Caspian	Edmund	Dragon
Drinian	Seapeople	

A Narnia Quiz

1 Fur coats.
2 A cat.
3 A lion (Aslan).
4 A new sewing-machine.
5 A hansom cab.
6 A stone knife.
7 A badger.
8 Through a picture.
9 He dresses the donkey up in a lion-skin.
10 A robin.
11 Puddleglum the Marsh-wiggle.
12 Mr Tumnus and Giant Rumblebuffin.
13 Shasta.
14 Strawberry.
15 A wolf.
16 The *Dawn Treader*.
17 The White Witch (Jadis).
18 Guinea-pigs.
19 Tash.
20 King Caspian.

Answers

Over the hills to Cair Paravel

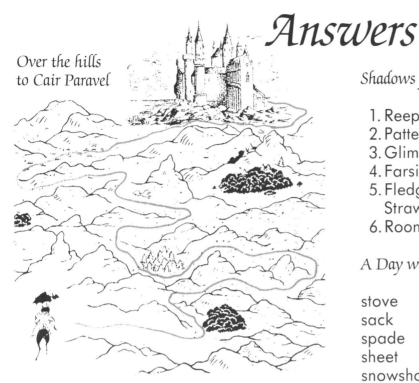

Shadows from Narnia

1. Reepicheep the Mouse
2. Pattertwig the Squirrel
3. Glimfeather the Owl
4. Farsight the Eagle
5. Fledge the flying horse (once called Strawberry)
6. Roonwhit the Centaur.

A Day with the Beavers

stove	saucepan
sack	sou'wester
spade	shovel
sheet	stool
snowshoes	spectacles
saw	sandwiches
shoes	shorts
shirt	socks
sewing machine	

Scrambled Narnian Names

CALORMEN	LANTERN WASTE
ANVARD	ARCHENLAND
GLASSWATER	ETTINSMOOR
ASLAN'S HOW	HARFANG
TASHBAAN	GALMA

ASLAN	ROON WIT
REEPICHEEP	CASPIAN
SHASTA	DIGORY
TRUMPKIN	RAMANDU

Back to Lamp Post

What's in a Name?

air, ant, art, ate, ban, banter, bar, bare, barn, bath, bathe, batten, batter, bean, bear, beat, been, beer, beet, beneath, beret bier, bin, birth, bit, bite, biter, bitten, brain, brat, breath, breathe, brine, eat, ear, earth, eaten, either, enter, entire, entreat, hair, hare, hart, hat, hate, hatter, hear, heart, heat, heater, here, heir, hen, hint, hire, hit, inherit, ire, irate, near, neat, neither, nib, nit nitrate, rain, ran, rat, rate, rib, rite, tab, tan, tar, tear, teat, teen, teeth, ten, tent, than, that, the, then, there, thin, tier, tin, tire, train, trait, treat, tree, tribe, trite

Racing Through Narnia

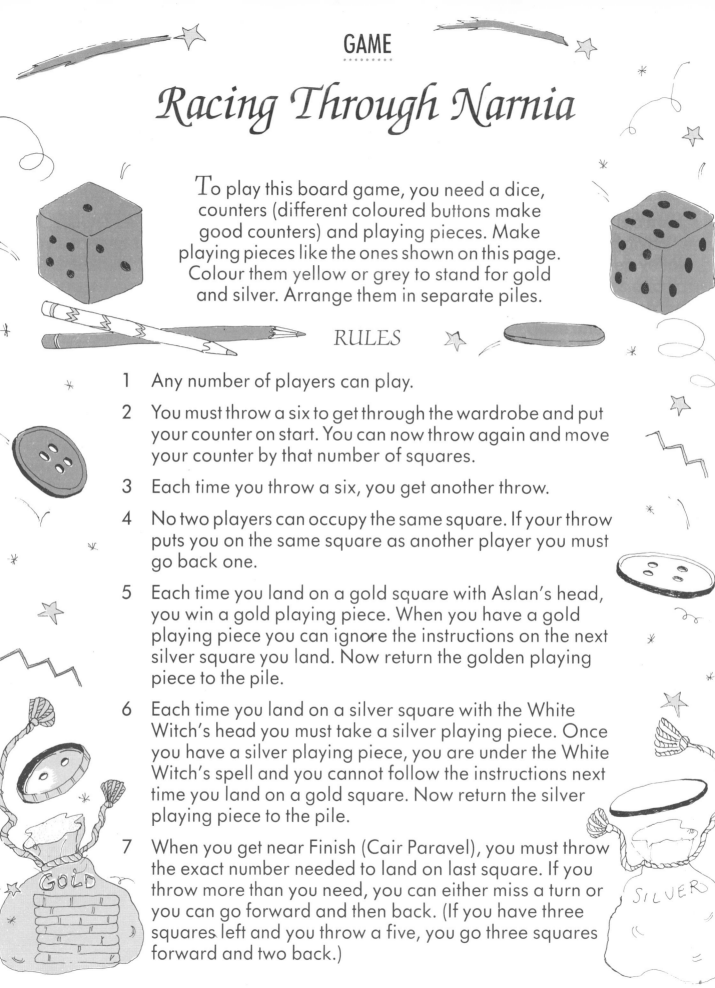

To play this board game, you need a dice, counters (different coloured buttons make good counters) and playing pieces. Make playing pieces like the ones shown on this page. Colour them yellow or grey to stand for gold and silver. Arrange them in separate piles.

RULES

1. Any number of players can play.

2. You must throw a six to get through the wardrobe and put your counter on start. You can now throw again and move your counter by that number of squares.

3. Each time you throw a six, you get another throw.

4. No two players can occupy the same square. If your throw puts you on the same square as another player you must go back one.

5. Each time you land on a gold square with Aslan's head, you win a gold playing piece. When you have a gold playing piece you can ignore the instructions on the next silver square you land. Now return the golden playing piece to the pile.

6. Each time you land on a silver square with the White Witch's head you must take a silver playing piece. Once you have a silver playing piece, you are under the White Witch's spell and you cannot follow the instructions next time you land on a gold square. Now return the silver playing piece to the pile.

7. When you get near Finish (Cair Paravel), you must throw the exact number needed to land on last square. If you throw more than you need, you can either miss a turn or you can go forward and then back. (If you have three squares left and you throw a five, you go three squares forward and two back.)